Disassembly

Steve Yockey

A SAMUEL FRENCH ACTING EDITION

SAMUELFRENCH.COM
SAMUELFRENCH-LONDON.CO.UK

DISASSEMBLY premiered at Impact Theatre (Melissa Hillman, Artistic Director; Cheshire Isaacs, Managing Director) at LaVal's Subterranean Theatre in Berkeley, California on May 6, 2011. The performance was directed by Desdemona Chiang, with sets by Anne Kendall, costumes by Ashley Rogers, properties by Tunuviel Luv-Gulamani, lights by Jax Steager, sound by Colin Trevor, and fight choreography by Desdemona Chiang. The cast was as follows:

ELLEN	Kathryn Zdan
EVAN / NARRATOR	Nick Trengrove
DIANE	Marissa Keltie
TESSA	Dina Percia
STANLEY	Seth Thygesen
JEROME / FOX	Timothy Redmond
MIRABELLE / CROW	Andrea Snow

DISASSEMBLY opened at Action/Adventure Theatre Company (Noah Dunham, Artistic Director) in Portland, Oregon on May 23, 2013. The performance was directed by Noah Dunham, with sets by Michael Miranda, costumes by Jade Harris, properties by Greta Pauley West, lights by Laura Fraley, sound by Devon Wade Granmo, and fight choreography by Kristen Mun. The cast was as follows:

ELLEN	Noelle Eaton
EVAN / NARRATOR	James Luster
DIANE	Jai Lavette
TESSA	Cecily Crow
STANLEY	Pat Moran
JEROME / FOX	Evan Ward
MIRABELLE / CROW	Greta Pauley West

CHARACTERS

ELLEN – A woman; deeply concerned for her brother, seemingly "normal" except for the inappropriate laughter, singing seizures, and lapses into extreme violence

EVAN / NARRATOR – A man; Ellen's brother, with a good attitude, a generous smile and a lot of unexplained injuries, or at least very poorly explained injuries

DIANE – A woman; Evan's fiancée, surface pretty, surface nice, making it through, but fed-up and breaking, trying her best to work it out

TESSA – A woman; all in black, very put together, overly polite, laughing at herself, past the point where death has any discernable impact

STANLEY – A man; sweet, caring, almost like a big teddy bear, with a healthy dose of psychotically jealous stalker underneath

JEROME / FOX – A man; Ellen's sometime boyfriend, very quiet, very tense, not very nice, but very much in love with the idea of love

MIRABELLE / CROW – A woman; Ellen and Evan's neighbor, she chews gum, she has cats, real and imagined, and a lot of attitude, somehow, oddly alluring

AUTHOR'S NOTES

[ ] indicate overlapping dialogue.

The Fox and Crow could be anything from small hand puppets to large marionettes operated by Jerome and Mirabelle or, more likely, they are represented simply and in an iconic fashion by the actors with a change in physicality and some ears, a tail, or a beak for good measure.

A Fox once saw a Crow fly off with a piece of cheese in its beak and settle on a branch of a tree. "That's for me, as I am a Fox," he thought and swiftly made his way to the foot of the tree. "Good day to you, Crow," he called up to her. "How very well you are looking today: how glossy your feathers; how bright your eyes. I feel certain your voice must surpass that of other birds, just as your fine figure does; let me hear but one song from you that I may greet you as the true Queen of Birds." The Crow, beguiled by the compliments, lifted up her head and began to caw her best. But the very moment she opened her mouth the piece of cheese fell to the ground, only to be snapped up by the Fox. "That will do," said the Fox. "That was all I wanted. In exchange for your cheese I will give you a piece of advice for the future: do not trust flatterers."

– an Aesop's Fable

(Afternoon. The dimly lit living room of a spacious but simply furnished apartment. **ELLEN** *sits on the couch wringing her hands.)*

(A small hallway is situated just outside the door to the apartment.)

(Off to the side in a small playing area that is much brighter, the **NARRATOR***, the* **FOX** *and the* **CROW** *stand on stage. As they begin,* **ELLEN***'s attention is drawn to their story. She watches and is captivated.)*

(The **NARRATOR** *tells his story. The* **FOX** *and the* **CROW** *act it all out very simply and cleanly.)*

NARRATOR. Once there was a Fox.

(The **FOX** *bows.)*

And a Crow.

(The **CROW** *curtseys.)*

And one day, the Fox saw the Crow fly off with a piece of cheese in her beak and settle down nicely on the branch of a tree. The Crow was, of course, going to eat the cheese, as crows are wont to do. But the Fox had a different plan.

FOX. That's for me, as I am a Fox.

NARRATOR. Said the Fox as he swiftly made his way to the foot of the tree.

FOX. Good day to you, Crow.

NARRATOR. He called up to her.

CROW. Mm hm.

FOX. How very well you are looking today.

(The **CROW** *giggles.)*

NARRATOR. And the Crow giggled.

CROW. Mm hm.

FOX. How glossy your feathers; how bright your eyes.

    (*The* **CROW** *bashfully demurs a bit.*)

NARRATOR. And the Crow blushed.

CROW. Mm hm.

FOX. I feel certain your voice must surpass that of other birds, just as your fine figure does; let me hear but one song, one joyous, clarion, brilliant, magical song from you that I may greet you as the true Queen of Birds.

NARRATOR. And the Crow, beguiled by the compliments of the Fox, lifted up her head and began to caw her best.

CROW. Caw!

    (*The* **CROW** *lets out a caw and drops the cheese. It falls into the waiting hands of the* **FOX.***)*

NARRATOR. But the very moment she opened her mouth the piece of cheese fell to the ground, only to be snapped up by the Fox.

FOX. That will do.

NARRATOR. Said the Fox.

CROW. That's not fair!

NARRATOR. Said the Crow.

FOX. No, it's not.

NARRATOR. Said the Fox.

CROW. What about all those nice things you said to me?

NARRATOR. Said the Crow.

FOX. This is all I wanted.

NARRATOR. Said the Fox.

FOX. But in exchange for your delicious cheese I will give you a piece of advice for the future: everyone lies and you'd better get used to it.

CROW. What?

NARRATOR. Said the Crow as she ruffled her feathers.

FOX. Mm hm, especially to get what they want. Everyone lies and you'd better get [used to it.]

CROW. [That's not the] moral; the moral is never trust flatterers.

FOX. Is it?

NARRATOR. Asked the fox, licking his chops.

CROW. Yes.

NARRATOR. Said the crow.

FOX. I guess we'll see about that.

> *(As the **FOX** eats the cheese with a smile and the **CROW** crosses her wings in a huff, **TESSA** and **STANLEY** appear in the small hallway just outside the door to the apartment. Notably, **TESSA** is in a black skirt, black turtleneck and carries a black purse. Nothing fancy, just all black.)*

> *(As they reach the door, the **NARRATOR**, **FOX** and **CROW** disappear from the stage and their area dims as lights pulse up on the apartment and hallway. **STANLEY** is about to knock…)*

TESSA. Stanley, wait.

STANLEY. Are you all right?

TESSA. Oh I'm fine, fine. Just let me get myself together for a minute.

STANLEY. Do you need anything?

TESSA. No, no. I'm fine. Just let me, I [mean…]

> *(**MIRABELLE** rounds the corner on the way to her apartment. She's carrying a stuffed cat. She's not carrying it like it's real; she just has a stuffed cat.)*

MIRABELLE. [Huh.] Maybe you two don't need to be standing in the hall like that.

TESSA. Oh, no, we're going to see our friend Ellen, this [is her…]

MIRABELLE. [Maybe you] two don't need to be standing in the hall like that.

STANLEY. Excuse me?

MIRABELLE. You're not excused you pair of hall standers standing in the hallway so other people can't get down the hall because of all your standing, the two of you, and maybe you could think about that the next time you just wanna stand in somebody else's hallway, somebody else's narrow hallway, in somebody else's building like a bunch of hall standers standing around with all the time in the world because you don't have all the time, you take other people's time in someone else's building where other people need to get down the hall.

TESSA. I'm, I'm sorry.

MIRABELLE. But look…you're still standing here.

>*(Pause. There is an awkward silence. **MIRABELLE** stares at them. She exits.)*

TESSA. Good grief.

>*(**TESSA** smoothes out her skirt, checks her sleeves, touches her hair as if making sure everything is where it's supposed to be. After a moment of this…)*

STANLEY. You look beautiful Tessa.

>*(She laughs reflexively.)*

You do.

TESSA. That's sweet honey, not right now okay.

STANLEY. I love [you.]

TESSA. [Shhh.]

STANLEY. But I've been trying to tell you…

>*(**TESSA** brushes past **STANLEY** and knocks on the door, interrupting him. **ELLEN** flies to answer it.)*

ELLEN. Thank you so much for coming, Tessa! Come in, [come in.]

TESSA. [Ellen] honey, you sounded [so…]

STANLEY. [Is he] okay?

>*(They enter. **JEROME** appears in the hallway as **ELLEN** closes the door. He stands looking at the door.)*

ELLEN. I think so, thank you for coming too Stanley. I think he's fine, it was all just so jarring, he's the only family I've got now, you know? And we're twins, did you know that?

TESSA. I think maybe I did.

ELLEN. It's like I can feel it more when he's, it sounds stupid. I probably didn't need to call you but I didn't know who to call besides Jerome and he wasn't answering, which is so typical, and Evan's fiancée Diane is already here and she's so much better in a crisis but I had to call someone and I'm sorry if interrupted your day [but I didn't…]

TESSA. [Don't worry] about that, I'm glad you called.

ELLEN. I knew you'd come. Somebody had to come.

TESSA. Here we are honey.

STANLEY. So he was stabbed?

> (**DIANE** *enters from the bedroom carrying a small trash bag that's pretty clearly full of bloody handy wipes and paper towels, wiping the hair from her face. Her hands have dried blood on them.*)

ELLEN. How is he?

DIANE. He's fine. He's sore, just let him rest. I tried to clean up the bathroom.

ELLEN. Oh my god Diane you probably saved his life.

DIANE. Let's not get all crazy about it, all right?

ELLEN. I'm not; it was terrifying.

DIANE. Yes it was.

ELLEN. Are you sure we shouldn't call the police?

DIANE. Evan says no police. I told him we should call. Trust me.

> (*She exits.* **JEROME** *exits back down the hall.*)

TESSA. You didn't call the police?

ELLEN. No.

STANLEY. If my brother went out for a jog and got stabbed, I think I'd call [the police.]

TESSA. [Honey, are] you at least taking him to the hospital?

ELLEN. He says no. He never goes. No insurance.

STANLEY. [Now, that's just…]

TESSA. [Honey, doesn't] [he…?]

ELLEN. [I know, I know,] but he's so accident prone, ever since we were little. Always getting hurt, oddly hurt, freak things like this.

STANLEY. Really?

ELLEN. No insurance company will take a chance on him. He has the worst luck.

STANLEY. You make your own luck.

ELLEN. Excuse me?

STANLEY. It's not my place to, I mean, I just think for the most part that people control their own fate. So, you know, you make your own luck.

ELLEN. No, no people don't. If you make your own luck Evan wouldn't be bleeding from the shoulder. He has bad luck.

STANLEY. I didn't mean, that's not what [I meant.]

ELLEN. [He has] bad luck.

TESSA. I understand what you're saying Ellen. I certainly know a thing or two about bad luck.

ELLEN. Yes you do. Oh no, I didn't [mean to…]

TESSA. [I'm fine;] it's fine. Look at me; I'm not upset at all. You've been there for me when I needed you, right? So let me be here for you right now.

> (**DIANE** *enters again and sits down. She is putting her hair back into place, fixing herself up.*)

STANLEY. I'm really surprised no one has called the police.

TESSA. Ellen explained that [Stanley.]

STANLEY. [Not really,] I mean she did, you did, but it [seems like…]

ELLEN. [Evan said] not to call. I don't know, [maybe we…]

DIANE. [Wow. I mean] really, wow, you practically have to scrub to the bone with that liquid soap to get all the blood off your hands. I bandaged up his shoulder with stuff from the medical kit, I don't think it was very bad. I don't really know what bad is, but with Evan I've seen worse. Oh, I'm sorry, I didn't even…

(She stretches out her hand to **STANLEY**.*)*

TESSA. Oh.

DIANE. I'm Diane, Evan's fiancée. You're friends of Ellen's?

*(***STANLEY** *looks at her hand.)*

I really did wash all of the blood off.

ELLEN. This is my best friend from the office Tessa and her friend Stanley.

STANLEY. Not exactly her ["friend"…]

*(***TESSA** *jumps in and shakes* **DIANE***'s hand.)*

TESSA. [Nice to] meet you. Sounds like you saved the day.

DIANE. Or something like that.

ELLEN. It was crazy, Tessa. I was napping on the couch, I'm so worthless on the weekends, and all of the sudden I heard this commotion, shouting and knocking around, Diane was trying to help Evan into the bedroom and she was holding her sweater over the wound so that, that, that all of the blood wouldn't, so much blood from just a…

(She starts to rock and hum a little bit. **DIANE** *freezes, then slowly, cool and direct…)*

DIANE. Ellen? Ellen what about my sweater?

(Pause. **ELLEN** *continues to rock and hum.)*

Ellen. What about my sweater?

*(***ELLEN** *snaps back into focus.)*

ELLEN. Oh Diane, your favorite sweater.

DIANE. I can get another sweater.

ELLEN. It was beautiful.

DIANE. I can get another one.

(EVAN enters. Shirtless, he has gauze over his shoulder held in place by thick, white medical tape. He has a very prominent scar on his abdomen and various marks and bruises; life hasn't been easy. But he's smiling.)

TESSA. Oh no…

EVAN. I'm, uh, I didn't realize there were [other people…]

(Before he can go, ELLEN is up and throwing a hug around him, seemingly oblivious to his injury.)

ELLEN. [I'm so] glad you're okay, I was so afraid that [you might…]

EVAN. [Ow, ow, Ellen,] ow, let go. I'm okay. Let me go get dressed.

ELLEN. This is Tessa and her friend Stanley.

STANLEY. I'm actually more [of her…]

TESSA. [Nice to] meet you. I'm glad you're okay.

EVAN. Thank you.

ELLEN. They came over because I didn't know who to call.

EVAN. Okay. Thanks.

STANLEY. You were jogging?

EVAN. Um, yes, yes I was, same route I always take. It was just bizarre, the guy came out of nowhere, I think, I don't really know because he was behind me obviously, and I guess he got scared because he didn't take anything. Almost seems like it didn't even happen, except for this of course. But Diane handled everything amazingly, like always. She's pretty fantastic putting up with me, always knows what to do.

DIANE. I do what I can.

EVAN. If she'd known when we met, I'm not sure she would've signed up for such a labor-intensive job.

(DIANE shrugs with an awkward laugh.)

DIANE. Too late now.

(He kisses DIANE. It is a truly felt kiss for both of them.)

EVAN. Everything's gonna be fine though. If I can survive this...

> *(He motions to the scar on his abdomen.)*

Then I'm pretty much indestructible.

STANLEY. What happened [there?]

TESSA. [Stanley,] shhh.

ELLEN. He doesn't mind talking about it, do you?

EVAN. Well, actually if you guys don't [mind...]

DIANE. [No, no,] why don't you tell them Evan.

> *(EVAN smiles at her. She smiles back at him. The smiles aren't really smiles.)*

EVAN. Okay, well, it's kind of embarrassing. Actually I was drunk one night when I was home from college and I fell out of second floor window. Onto a picket fence.

STANLEY. Oh my god!

EVAN. It sounds worse than it actually was. Or maybe not. It was pretty bad.

DIANE. Now Evan, I wouldn't think you could fall on just one point of a picket fence.

EVAN. You can.

DIANE. Seems almost impossible.

EVAN. Nope.

DIANE. Seems almost like something completely made up.

EVAN. And yet, Diane, you know that's what happened. I was climbing on the roof, trying to sneak in an upstairs window so my folks wouldn't know I was drunk. I got one leg in and then, just, leaned back. I kinda' torqued around in the air so I was facing the ground and then bam.

> *(ELLEN and EVAN both clap their hands together to punctuate the moment.)*

It probably looked like something out of a horror movie, but mercifully I don't remember much after that.

ELLEN. Of course I don't remember any of this; I'm always amazed when he tells this story. I was asleep in my room; I sleep like the dead, and didn't wake up until the ambulance sirens were coming down the block. So useless.

EVAN. Naw, she came to the hospital every day after classes, didn't you? And you brought those little animal puppets from [home.]

ELLEN. [Oh!]

EVAN. All of these animal puppets and she'd put on little skits for me.

STANLEY. And you were in college?

TESSA. Stop it, Stanley; that sounds adorable.

ELLEN. They weren't skits; they were those short animal stories. Fables? Aesop's fables. Oh, I just loved Aesop's fables. You can't even imagine, Tessa. I loved them.

EVAN. She did.

ELLEN. My favorite was "The Fox and The Crow."

TESSA. Oh, now, I think I remember that one, something about cheese? They were fighting over cheese?

STANLEY. Sure, cheese.

EVAN. It's the one about flattery.

ELLEN. It's about lying.

EVAN. It's about flattery, beware of flattery.

ELLEN. Huh, I guess sometimes I got the endings wrong. It didn't matter, it's not a big deal, I mean morals are always changing anyway.

DIANE. The morals don't change, Ellen. That's the [whole point.]

EVAN. [Listen, I was] so drugged up, I couldn't tell. They were just little puppet shows to me. Oh, and sometimes we'd play chess.

ELLEN. You don't know how to play chess. We played checkers and I won every game.

> *(She repeatedly, teasingly, pokes* **EVAN** *in his injured shoulder.)*

EVAN. Ow, ow, okay, well that's not how I remember it, but like I said, I was on a lot of drugs. Those visits were great, until something went wrong with my ventilator. After that, I wasn't allowed to have visitors in the Intensive Care Unit anymore.

ELLEN. That was sad.

TESSA. What's that other, oh, you don't mind my asking do you?

EVAN. Which one?

TESSA. Just, that mark there?

EVAN. This one? Scissor accident.

TESSA. And that one?

EVAN. Um, oh, I crashed a golf cart.

TESSA. Fascinating.

DIANE. It is fascinating.

EVAN. Diane.

ELLEN. Oh, you should be resting. Do you need anything?

STANLEY. The police maybe?

TESSA. Stanley, stop it.

DIANE. He needs to lie down; he lost blood. And some juice, he needs to drink some orange juice [or something.]

ELLEN. [I'll get it,] I'll bring it to you.

EVAN. These ladies take such great care of me, huh?

ELLEN. We do our best.

(ELLEN exits to the kitchen.)

DIANE. I do my best.

EVAN. You're the best thing that's ever happened to me, Diane. I know it. And I just, I hope this morning wasn't too scary for you.

DIANE. I'm okay.

EVAN. You sure?

DIANE. Yep, look at me. I'm fine.

EVAN. Love you.

(**EVAN** *kisses* **DIANE**'s *forehead and exits. She looks after him for a moment and then snaps back to* **TESSA** *and* **STANLEY**.)

TESSA. Oh, you two are just adorable.

STANLEY. *(Under his breath…)* I don't know if [adorable is…]

TESSA. [Stanley,] please.

DIANE. So you work with Ellen?

TESSA. Yes. We're both tellers at the bank, the branch on Ponce, but I guess you [know that.]

DIANE. [And you're] friends?

TESSA. Yes.

DIANE. Close friends?

TESSA. Um, yes? I don't know, I think so.

DIANE. Huh. I think work and sleep must be the only times that Ellen and Evan are ever actually apart.

TESSA. Oh.

DIANE. And this is your boyfriend?

TESSA. *(With an involuntary laugh…)* Oh no, this is Stanley. He's one of my best friends. We've known each other since, well I don't even know.

STANLEY. Kindergarten.

TESSA. Such a long time, Stanley's my rock. But actually, I don't date men.

DIANE. Oh. I see.

(**STANLEY** *and* **TESSA** *laugh.*)

TESSA. Oh no, no, not like that, I don't mean I don't date men, I mean I don't date. At all. I've had a peculiar kind of, well not peculiar, that's not the word. I've had a surprising run of misfortune with men.

STANLEY. You don't have to get into this right now Tessa.

TESSA. I'm not getting into anything.

DIANE. What does that mean, misfortune?

TESSA. Well, maybe that's not the right word either.

DIANE. I mean, I can relate to misfortune I think. I'm exhausted all the time and, frankly, I'm half surprised that Evan isn't already dead at this point.

(**TESSA** *laughs.*)

TESSA. I'm sorry, I didn't mean to laugh. I'm not… I've been engaged four times.

DIANE. Whoa. No, not "whoa," I'm sorry. It's just surprising; you seem so young.

TESSA. I am.

STANLEY. She is.

DIANE. That's definitely misfortune.

(**TESSA** *laughs again.*)

TESSA. I keep laughing; it's not you. It's just how I've been able to keep moving, you know? Honey, I've been engaged four times and all of those men have died.

DIANE. Are you serious?

(**ELLEN** *passes through with a glass.*)

ELLEN. We didn't have orange juice so I had to make lemonade and I know it's not the same Diane but it's all we had.

(*She is gone.*)

STANLEY. That's probably enough Tessa, I don't want you to get upset.

TESSA. No, I'm not upset. You don't mind do you, Diane? Oh I hope not, it's just one of those things that's too insane to be true but it's had such a huge impact on how I meet, or how I interact with people that I've found it's easier to just get it out of the way right at the beginning.

DIANE. That's…okay.

TESSA. Once this is out of the way, there won't be any odd little secrets to stumble upon. Just me, what's left of me anyway, so silly.

(**TESSA** *laughs.*)

DIANE. Sure.

TESSA. And you know, Ellen has been there for me the last two times in such a caring and generous way.

DIANE. Ellen has?

TESSA. She's so attentive.

DIANE. Is she?

STANLEY. And I'm there, too.

TESSA. Stanley's always there. I don't know what I'd do without him.

STANLEY. I'm right here.

(TESSA *smiles.*)

DIANE. Four times, I can't begin to imagine what that must be like.

TESSA. Oh, it's like your life is a funeral.

DIANE. Oh.

TESSA. Mm hm, one long funeral march, with all of the trappings. I say life, but this has all happened in what? The last six years I suppose.

STANLEY. That's right.

TESSA. Seems like longer, but it's not. Time kind of slows down. And inside the never-ending funeral, once all of the crying is done, you start to notice things, like the time that must have gone into the woodwork on the mantle above the coffin, or the craftsmanship of a leather bound bible. Or how food always tastes better at a wake because it's comforting. And then your perspective starts to shift. Because it has to really. Things become funny, or maybe numb. But mostly just funny. And you see how ephemeral every moment can be. That's the only way I know how to explain it, which doesn't really explain it, but there it is. Oh just listen to me go on and on in the middle of somebody else's crisis.

(JEROME *appears again and knocks on the door.*)

DIANE. No, it's fine, really. Just, um, hold on a second.

*(She answers it. **JEROME** enters, but only a step. **DIANE** leaves him in the open doorway and returns to her seat.)*

JEROME. Where's Ellen?

DIANE. Hello Jerome, come on in.

JEROME. Where's Ellen?

DIANE. She's with Evan?

JEROME. Why's she with Evan?

DIANE. She's in the bedroom.

JEROME. Why's she in the bedroom?

DIANE. She's with Evan.

JEROME. Why's she with Evan?

DIANE. Jesus, because they're doing interpretive dance, Jerome. We've had a kinda' crazy few hours, could you please come in and close the door.

JEROME. It's not your apartment and you can't tell me what to do.

(He comes in and closes the door.)

DIANE. Thanks for that.

JEROME. Don't thank me. I did it because Ellen likes it when I close the door not because you told me to. And I'm not particularly thrilled that you haven't told me, simply and plainly, what Ellen and Evan are doing in the bedroom. I've got things to say to Ellen. And I don't care about interpretive dance, I don't even like interpretive dance, and I don't believe that's what they're doing back there because you're very evasive, Diane, I see that about you, how you talk around things and I hate it and who are they?

DIANE. *(With a weary sigh…)* Ask them.

JEROME. Who are you?

STANLEY. My name is Stanley [and this is…]

JEROME. [Who are] they?

DIANE. Fuck. Jerome this is Tessa and this is Stanley. They're friends of Ellen.

JEROME. No they're not. If that were true I would know them, I would know you. I'm Ellen's boyfriend and I've never met you.

TESSA. I didn't know Ellen had a boyfriend.

DIANE. She doesn't.

JEROME. She does.

DIANE. She doesn't.

JEROME. Ellen called me and she was crying.

> (**MIRABELLE** *knocks on the door. Really more of a banging.*)

DIANE. It's like Grand Central around here. Not you two, I'm not talking about you two.

> (**DIANE** *pushes past* **JEROME** *to answer the door.* **MIRABELLE** *puts on a huge smile and is almost plastic in her niceties.*)

MIRABELLE. Oh hi Diane.

DIANE. Mirabelle.

MIRABELLE. How are you?

DIANE. Busy.

MIRABELLE. Oh I know you must be with all of these guests hanging around the hallway, getting in the way, but I wondered if you had a quick second?

DIANE. As you mentioned, we do have company [so maybe...]

MIRABELLE. [There's smoke] coming out of the bedroom window. That bedroom. Evan's bedroom, that one right there.

DIANE. Smoke?

MIRABELLE. From Evan's bedroom. I know which one is his. Which bedroom.

DIANE. You do so enjoy reminding me.

MIRABELLE. Yes. Yes I do.

DIANE. You do.

MIRABELLE. Mm hm I said I do, so there's smoke, and because of the lovely, architecturally sound U-shaped construction of our building, with the narrow hallways full of your guests, that smoke is drifting into my kitchen. And it's making my cats cough.

DIANE. I don't think there's any smoke.

MIRABELLE. You don't think?

DIANE. No.

MIRABELLE. You don't think.

DIANE. Okay, I don't have time for this.

MIRABELLE. Please do something about the smoke.

DIANE. I will do my level best to stop the imaginary smoke.

MIRABELLE. Mm hm, and keep the noise down if your little party gets any bigger. And tell Evan I said that I'll see him soon; can you do that?

DIANE. Yep.

JEROME. No one likes you.

MIRABELLE. Huh, no one likes you either, baby.

(She exits casually. **DIANE** *closes the door and crosses the room.)*

JEROME. No one likes you either more!!

DIANE. Jesus.

STANLEY. We ran into that woman on the stairs. She's not very nice, is she?

TESSA. Stanley.

STANLEY. She's not.

DIANE. No, she's not Stanley.

JEROME. You shouldn't let her talk like that to me Diane.

DIANE. You talk like that to her, Jerome.

JEROME. It's not the same, Diane. I've got things to say. You don't even care.

DIANE. Nope, I'm not your mother, Jerome. Would you two excuse me for a minute?

(She exits into the bedroom.)

*(***JEROME*** stands awkwardly, not speaking.* **STANLEY** *and* **TESSA** *look at him. He backs away a bit. Pause.)*

JEROME. I can juggle.

TESSA. Oh?

STANLEY. Really?

JEROME. Not right now though, I don't have my things right now.

TESSA. Oh.

STANLEY. Really.

> *(Pause. They turn their attention away from* **JEROME.***)*

How long do you think we should stay?

TESSA. Well I didn't really get to speak with Ellen very much yet.

STANLEY. But it seems like everything is okay.

TESSA. Just be a little patient, all right?

STANLEY. No, I am. I mean yes. I'm not in a hurry. Take some time with your friend.

TESSA. I really appreciate it.

STANLEY. Whatever you need. It's just, it seems like a lot is going on, doesn't it?

TESSA. Yes, but just relax.

JEROME. I wasn't lying. I really can juggle.

> *(***DIANE*** *crosses through and exits into the kitchen.* **EVAN**, *still shirtless, bandaged and beaten, follows her carrying a glass of lemonade.)*

EVAN. It was one cigarette, or two maybe.

DIANE. Fuck that.

EVAN. Come on, I just got stabbed.

DIANE. That's a bullshit excuse.

EVAN. Getting stabbed is a bullshit excuse?

> *(They are gone.* **ELLEN** *enters.* **JEROME** *backs up even more.)*

ELLEN. Um, they're just going to talk in the kitchen for a minute. I'm not supposed to let him do that, the smoking thing. Sorry to leave you out here like that. Do you need anything?

STANLEY. We're good.

JEROME. I want some coffee.

ELLEN. Oh! Oh, Jerome. I didn't know you were here.

JEROME. I got your message.

ELLEN. Good.

JEROME. I didn't listen to it, I just heard you crying so I came over. Are you okay?

ELLEN. Evan was stabbed.

JEROME. Did he die?

ELLEN. What? No, of course not, you just saw him. What kind of question is that?

> (**JEROME** *crosses to* **ELLEN** *and hugs her. It is possibly the most awkward hug ever offered, but she warmly returns the embrace.*)

JEROME. So he's not dead.

ELLEN. Everything's okay now.

JEROME. Can I have some coffee?

ELLEN. Yes you can have some coffee.

JEROME. Will you make it?

ELLEN. Yes.

JEROME. Do they need anything?

STANLEY. We're still good.

ELLEN. I'm sorry Tessa, I'll be right back. Come on, Jerome.

> (*She takes his hand and they exit into the kitchen.*)

TESSA. Maybe you're right, maybe we [should…]

> (**EVAN** *and* **DIANE** *enter. She sits down again, he continues to the bedroom.*)

EVAN. [Sorry, sorry] you two, I still need a shirt.

DIANE. And put more tape on the bandage.

> (*He's gone. Pause. Then in a burst…*)

And if you're smoking in there I will kick your ass!

STANLEY. Is it, Diane, would it be better if we left?

TESSA. Just got out of your [way, or…?]

DIANE. [It's always] like this. Not just like this, but similar. So exhausting. It's actually nice to have some new people around. But if you'd rather go, that's fine.

(STANLEY *begins to rise, but* TESSA *holds on to his arm and stops him.*)

TESSA. No, we're fine.

DIANE. Trust me when I tell you that I understand if you want to go.

(STANLEY *starts to get up, but* TESSA *nonchalantly pulls him back down onto the couch.*)

TESSA. Trust me when I tell you we're fine, right Stanley?

STANLEY. Absolutely.

DIANE. All right. I'm being a terrible host, or I guess Ellen's being a terrible host, would you like something to drink or eat? I feel like the refrigerator is always empty, but there are eggs. I could whip something up?

STANLEY. No eggs.

TESSA. He means, "No, thank you."

DIANE. What's wrong with eggs? Is that a weird thing to offer, it's weird, right?

STANLEY. Just don't ask about the eggs.

TESSA. He's just being silly. All of this death stuff, well not all of it, but after Jerry I think, Jerry was my second fiancé, after he died I became a vegetarian. And then a vegan, I got a little obsessive about it. But I've moved through that and I'm back to eating pretty much anything.

DIANE. What does that have to do with eggs?

STANLEY. Oh God.

TESSA. Well, I could never really get back into eggs. I don't know. Whenever I try to eat anything that has egg in it I feel like I can actually taste the little dead baby chicks. I can feel myself chewing up their little unformed bodies. And clearly that's not something anyone wants to be thinking.

DIANE. Wow.

STANLEY. Indeed.

DIANE. That's kind of awful.

(TESSA *laughs again.*)

TESSA. I'm just silly about some things now. Morbid things, well, I can't tell what's morbid anymore so I'm not the best judge of that I suppose. Anyway, enough of that. I think it's time for some girl talk, with you too of course, Stanley.

DIANE. Girl talk?

TESSA. So you and Evan, how long?

DIANE. Oh, um, two years. A little over two years.

TESSA. Aww, that's so great. That's a good amount of time. Isn't it Stanley?

(*She takes his hand unconsciously. He lights up.*)

STANLEY. Yes. Yes.

TESSA. I never could wait.

(*She pulls her hand away just as naturally.*)

And look how that turned out.

DIANE. I don't think, we haven't, I mean that it doesn't even feel like that long really. But we're both in the same place now, both excited. I really, really love him. More than I've ever loved anyone I think.

TESSA. It shows.

DIANE. Thank you.

STANLEY. How did he pop the question?

DIANE. Oh it's not a very good, it wasn't what you'd think of as romantic [necessarily.]

TESSA. [Oh, you,] [go on.]

STANLEY. [I'm sure it] was great.

DIANE. We were in the hospital, the emergency room.

(TESS *reflexively puts her hand on her chest and glances at* STANLEY *as his eyebrows perk up awkwardly.*)

TESSA. Oh?

DIANE. It was really sweet in the way that things are sweet around here I guess. He was having his jaw reset.

TESSA. Oh!

DIANE. It was pretty awful, I don't know if you've ever seen anything like that, but it's intense. Apparently he had planned to ask me before the "accident" and then he still went through with it. All of the doctors clapped. Of course, I had to verify everything once the morphine wore off and he was able to speak again, but he really meant it, he really meant it and I love him so much that I don't know how to not love him and soon I'll be a permanent part of all this…

(She is crying now. Not happy tears.)

TESSA. Oh honey, don't cry.

DIANE. No, no, I'm sorry. It was just scary this morning.

STANLEY. Random crime is the worst because there's no way to prepare yourself.

TESSA. That's so true. But it could have been worse, so [things aren't…]

DIANE. [I know it] could have been worse!

TESSA. Oh. Um…

(Pause. Awkward.)

DIANE. No, not, I didn't mean to yell. I don't know how to…

(She stops. Something changes in her. Something focuses.)

Look, Tessa, you're friends with Ellen?

TESSA. Yes.

DIANE. Does she ever, I mean, have you ever been around her during one of her "episodes?"

TESSA. I'm sorry?

DIANE. With the singing?

TESSA. I don't know what that means.

DIANE. You've never seen the singing?

TESSA. I don't think so.

DIANE. I'm afraid she's going to kill him.

STANLEY. What?

TESSA. Honey, I [don't…]

DIANE. [Listen,] if I don't do something, Ellen is going to kill Evan.

>   *(pause)*

TESSA. Is this some kind of joke?

>   (**MIRABELLE** *knocks on the door. Again, it's more of a banging.* **DIANE** *heads to the door and just before opening it…)*

DIANE. No. No it's not a joke.

>   *(She opens the door.)*

MIRABELLE. I'm back.

DIANE. Not a good time.

>   (**DIANE** *closes the door.* **MIRABELLE** *bangs again.* **DIANE** *opens…)*

Yes?

MIRABELLE. Don't say 'yes' to me like that?

DIANE. Yes?

MIRABELLE. First off, don't ever close the door in my face again you door closer closing doors on people who are being perfectly polite. I am not the one you want to close a door on, you and your hall standing pals. Second, can you quit all of this banging around? I hear you stomping on the floors.

DIANE. We're just sitting here.

MIRABELLE. I can hear it in the floor.

DIANE. You don't even live below us, you live around the corner.

MIRABELLE. And I can still hear it, so just imagine what the people underneath you are going through.

DIANE. We will keep it down.

MIRABELLE. Will you?

DIANE. Yes.

MIRABELLE. That'll be great.

DIANE. I'm so glad.

MIRABELLE. Is Evan here?

DIANE. No.

MIRABELLE. Evan! Can you come out [here?]

TESSA. [Ma'am, I] don't mean to be impolite, but we're kind of in the middle of something important, I think. Weren't we Diane?

DIANE. Yes.

MIRABELLE. "Ma'am?"

TESSA. Oh, no, I didn't [mean to...]

MIRABELLE. [No one] calls me "ma'am" because I am not old enough to be a "ma'am," do I look old enough to be a "ma'am?" And I'm not interested in whatever interests are in your silly pretty little head or if I interrupted your silly pretty little chat or what your silly pretty little brain thinks is too [important for...]

> (**STANLEY** *explodes. It's not a transformation. It comes out of nowhere. He jumps up and charges towards the door, pushing* **DIANE** *out of the way.*)

STANLEY. [Shut your fucking] mouth you stupid bitch! Don't you ever, ever talk to her that way! No one talks to her that way! If you even look at her with a cross eye one more time I will come to your place and take you apart starting with your fucking tongue! Now shut the fuck up and get out!

> (*He pushes her back into the hall roughly and slams the door. For a moment,* **MIRABELLE** *and* **STANLEY** *are both standing on either side of the door breathing heavy.* **DIANE** *and* **TESSA** *are very still.* **MIRABELLE** *exits quickly.* **STANLEY** *catches his breath. After a moment of this...*)

TESSA. Stanley?

STANLEY. I'm sorry.

TESSA. Take some deep breaths, all right?

STANLEY. I'm sorry. It's just very stressful, all of this and she shouldn't speak to Tessa that way. I'm sorry Diane, are you all, right?

DIANE. I'm…fine.

TESSA. Stanley, come and sit down.

> (*He does sit awkwardly next to her. She rubs his near shoulder.*)

You just need to cool down for a minute, right?

STANLEY. I'm sorry.

> (**EVAN** *enters from the bedroom. He's finally found a shirt.*)

EVAN. What was that yelling?

TESSA. Stanley [was just…]

DIANE. [Nothing.]

EVAN. Diane?

DIANE. It was nothing. You should be resting. All of this up and down can't be good for you. If we're not going to a hospital then you have to rest and give yourself a chance to heal.

EVAN. I want to know what's going on, I heard yelling.

STANLEY. I'm sorry.

DIANE. You need to go lie down.

EVAN. I'm not gonna do that until you answer me.

DIANE. Evan, you know that I love you, right?

EVAN. Of course I do.

DIANE. Evan, you love me too, right?

EVAN. You know I do, yes.

DIANE. Evan, do you trust me?

EVAN. Why do you keep saying my name like that?

DIANE. Evan, I was about to tell Ellen's friends my theory on how your sister is going to kill you.

> *(Pause. And it is lengthy. And it is awkward. After
> a moment,* **EVAN** *puts on the most incredibly false
> smile that has ever been managed.)*

EVAN. Diane, could I see you in the bedroom?

DIANE. I don't think I should leave Tessa [and Stanley...]

EVAN. [Could I see] you in the bedroom, please?

DIANE. Will you lie down while we talk?

EVAN. Bedroom.

DIANE. *(With another weary sigh...)* Yep.

> *(She exits with* **EVAN**. **STANLEY** *and* **TESSA** *are
> alone.)*

TESSA. Well this day is just a little bit out of control, isn't it?

STANLEY. I'm sorry.

TESSA. Please stop apologizing, Stanley. It was chivalrous. It was terrifying, but it was chivalrous. It's nice to know there are still men like you out there. And that should make you feel good. I'm glad you're here.

STANLEY. Really?

TESSA. Really.

STANLEY. I love you, Tessa.

TESSA. If you weren't here, I don't know what I would have done.

STANLEY. I love you.

TESSA. Everyone else seems to have gone a bit insane, right?

STANLEY. I love you.

> *(With a nervous laugh she springs up off the
> couch. It's almost as if she had been launched.)*

TESSA. Oh Stanley, why won't you just realize that I never respond to you when you say that because I can't respond to you when you say that?

STANLEY. I don't understand.

TESSA. Oh, I know.

STANLEY. I've known you practically my whole life. I've been in love with you since I was a little boy and I don't care how that sounds. When we met again in college, when I saw you, nothing had changed. I still loved you just as much as I did when we were little and I told myself "I won't let her get away again." I said that to myself out loud. And now I'm saying it to you. Out loud. Finally. And maybe I'm not every single thing you look for in a guy, I know I'm not, but no one will ever love you as much or as truly as I do.

> *(Pause.)*

TESSA. I'm touched.

STANLEY. Good.

TESSA. Maybe, and I'm saying maybe, maybe there was a time when something could have happened Stanley. I can give you that much.

STANLEY. Maybe?

TESSA. But not anymore.

STANLEY. Why?

TESSA. Stanley. Listen to me very clearly: I can't love anyone again and even if I could I wouldn't let myself love you because look at what happens to all of the men I love. Seriously, look at what happens, do you want to end up in a pine box?

STANLEY. That won't happen to me.

TESSA. It will, I know it will.

STANLEY. No.

TESSA. Or at the very least it might. And because there's no way to know I will not even entertain the idea. I won't ever let you in my heart that way, not even a crack, not even a sliver, not after already losing four men, four loves, four potential forevers. And you need to hear that I suppose. You really need to understand that.

STANLEY. But I'm here. I'm good. It's my turn.

TESSA. It doesn't work like that.

STANLEY. Oh.

(**STANLEY** *collapses into himself.*)

TESSA. And the worst, the absolute worst thing is that I know you feel that way. I've known for a long time and I've been selfish not telling you all of this flat out honey. For that I am sorry. But I don't know what I'd do without you and the idea of hurting you is, well, it's just too much. You mean too much, Stanley. And I didn't want to do this here obviously, in the midst of all this near-insanity, but you just push so hard sometimes.

(**STANLEY** *wipes away tears.*)

STANLEY. I don't mean to.

TESSA. I know that.

STANLEY. I just…love you so much I can't breathe sometimes.

TESSA. That's very sweet, honey. But it's not good. For you. Or me.

(*Pause.*)

I do appreciate you Stanley, I even love you if that's what you need to hear, I do. But it'll never be the way you want. I won't ever heal enough to love anyone that way again. Look at me: the universe uses me for sport and I wear black every single day and laugh about it. That funeral feeling I was trying to describe earlier? It applies to everything. Everyone. Even you.

(*They both sit but they do not look at each other.* **STANLEY** *seems to have gone completely blank. As if there's no one left inside him. After a moment, she takes his hand…*)

I'm sorry.

STANLEY. I'm sorry too.

(**ELLEN** *and* **JEROME** *enter from the kitchen.* **STANLEY** *and* **TESSA** *are still shell shocked from their unexpected, unintended chat.*)

ELLEN. Uh, did they just leave you two in here by yourselves?

STANLEY. [Yes.]

TESSA. [Yes.]

ELLEN. Well that wasn't very nice.

JEROME. Diane's not very nice.

ELLEN. Stop it, Jerome.

JEROME. She's not.

ELLEN. Stop. Now what have you two been up to?

STANLEY. [Nothing.]

TESSA. [Nothing.]

ELLEN. Oh, all right. Well, it's so great you came over Tessa, but I don't want you to feel trapped or anything?

TESSA. I don't.

JEROME. I have things to say Ellen, important things to say to you.

ELLEN. Not now, all right.

JEROME. But that's what you said in the kitchen.

ELLEN. Not now.

JEROME. Then can we go make out?

ELLEN. No.

STANLEY. Why does Diane think you're going to kill Evan?

TESSA. Stanley, [don't.]

STANLEY. [She told] us you're going to kill him.

ELLEN. What?

TESSA. Be mad at me if you need to but don't take it out on [anyone else.]

STANLEY. [She told us] she's afraid for his life. That she needs to rescue him from you.

ELLEN. Is that true, Tessa?

TESSA. Honey, today's been really hard on all of you, okay? Don't worry about it right now because she probably just meant [something else.]

JEROME. [I hate Diane.]

ELLEN. Why would she say that?

STANLEY. Why would she say that?

ELLEN. Why would she say that?

STANLEY. I'm asking you, why would she say that?

ELLEN. I don't know!!!! Evan's the most important thing in the world to me, he always has been, I'd never do anything, to, I'd never, I don't know why Diane would think something so awful, awful, Diane likes me, I'm likeable, look at me, I'm normal, I'm just, I would never do something so, I've been there, terrible, I'm the one who's been there for Evan for his entire life, violent, my entire life, every single horrifying, I wouldn't, awful, he can't ever, I need him, it won't ever, he needs me, he needs me, I would never, I'd never, never, never...

> (**ELLEN** *sits down and begins humming and rocking back and forth again.*)

TESSA. Are you happy now Stanley? Are you proud of yourself?

STANLEY. I didn't do anything.

JEROME. It's Diane's fault. I hate Diane.

TESSA. Ellen, are you okay?

> (**ELLEN** *jerks upright as if her body was lifted into a standing position. Her limbs at odd angles, her head askew, eye blank, she begins to sing. She begins in the middle of a song as if a needle has been dropped on a record. She is singing some kind of gospel power pop like "Shout to the Lord" or an equivalent. It's not loud, it's sung, but it's also jerky, impacted by shakes that periodically wrack her body.*)

JEROME. Oh no, no no [no no no...]

TESSA. [Ellen, honey,] what's [going on?]

STANLEY. [Tessa, maybe] step away from her.

TESSA. She's not going to hurt me for [God's sake.]

JEROME. [Diane! Diane] come out here! Diane!

> (*Her runs to get* **DIANE**. **ELLEN** *gets louder, her spasms more violent.* **TESSA** *looks to* **STANLEY**...)

TESSA. I don't know what to do?

(JEROME enters with DIANE.)

DIANE. Jesus, Ellen, twice in one day? Are you kidding me with this shit?!

TESSA. How can we help?

(DIANE yells over ELLEN's singing and theatrics.)

DIANE. There's nothing to help. This is what she does. It's a show. She's faking it. This is how she gets attention. This is how she scares everybody away from her brother. I'm not going anywhere Ellen. I'm not going anywhere!

(EVAN enters.)

EVAN. Oh fuck, which one is it? Which one is it [Diane?]

DIANE. [Go back] to bed, you should be [in bed.]

EVAN. [Which fucking] song is it?

STANLEY. Does it matter [what she's singing?]

TESSA. [How can you even] tell?

EVAN. Shut up, everyone.

DIANE. Evan, just [let her…]

EVAN. [Just shut] up for a minute. Let me try and…

(Everyone is quiet as ELLEN continues to haltingly sing, shout and lurch out the song while convulsing.)

Okay, okay…

(EVAN approaches ELLEN cautiously.)

DIANE. Don't get too close.

EVAN. You should know better, Diane.

DIANE. I do know better.

(As he approaches he begins to sing the same song ELLEN is singing. He sings it gently, beautifully. He sings along with her and the shaking begins to stop. ELLEN's voice begins to clarify, passing into lovely song. She and EVAN sing in harmony as her body loses its rigidity. For a moment, they are truly lovely in song as her eyes focus on him. Then she passes out and he catches her.)

EVAN. Somebody help me, Jerome, help me get her into the [bedroom.]

JEROME. [I can do] that.

(He rushes to help hold **ELLEN** *up.)*

EVAN. We just need to put her on the bed. She'll be out for a while.

TESSA. I'll, I'll come with you. Maybe a cool rag or, I don't know.

(They exit. **DIANE** *crashes into a chair.* **STANLEY** *sits on the couch.)*

STANLEY. That was, I don't even know the word, harrowing maybe?

DIANE. *(laughing)* Harrowing.

STANLEY. Or something like harrowing, definitely.

DIANE. You know what happens when he doesn't know the song? She loses it completely. I mean, off the charts. She breaks things, throws things. It gets really violent, incredibly violent. All while singing gospel pop songs.

STANLEY. I've never seen anything like it.

DIANE. This morning she stabbed Evan in the shoulder with a letter opener.

STANLEY. Diane, what?

DIANE. I don't even know where she got it. The scissors were her scissors. The golf cart thing? She hit him with her car. She never remembers any of it, claims to never remember. Oh, and that huge scar, the picket fence scar? She did that with a shovel when he was passed out drunk on the floor one night. He told me. And I've seen it. But he doesn't know how to do anything about, or he won't do anything about it. Everything's about her, keeping her safe, keeping her out of the mental ward and he thinks he'll just keep recovering, surviving. Until she finally kills him. I used to believe it, all of it. Not anymore. I think she does it for attention. I think she does it to scare people away so she can be the only person in his life. He's got this huge blind spot when it comes to her. I mean look at him: he's had a life of being torn to pieces trying to "protect" her. She's slowly taking him apart, a little bit at a time. A little, awful bit at a time. And I don't think she would do it on purpose, kill him I mean, but it might happen just the same. And I love him so much I just want to make it stop but I, oh, oh God, I shouldn't be saying all of this in [front of you.]

STANLEY. [No, please,] [it's fine.]

DIANE. [Oh Jesus, just] forget I said any of, just forget it.

> *(Pause. After a moment, **STANLEY** moves down the couch closer to **DIANE**'s chair. He is very calm. He is collected, gentle and soft spoken.)*

STANLEY. Diane, you don't know me well.

DIANE. I don't know you at all.

STANLEY. That's right, and I don't really know you.

DIANE. No.

STANLEY. But I want to say something to you.

DIANE. I don't know if I [can really…]

STANLEY. [I hope I can] say something to you and have you really hear me.

> *(She looks over at him and they connect. He is perfectly calm.)*

DIANE. What is it?

STANLEY. I want to say that I understand what you're talking about, when you say how much you love him, how much you want to keep him safe. There are people in the world who really do love in a way that is greater than all of the small tokens of romance that pass for love these days. And if your love for Evan is so strong that you need to act, need to keep him safe? Then you should.

DIANE. I do.

STANLEY. When I said that I've known Tessa since kindergarten that was no exaggeration. I loved her the moment I saw her. I loved her all of the time in between childhood and when I met her again. No one can love her the way I can. But when I found her again, she was engaged, her first engagement. That couldn't be right though, could it? We belong together. So I went to talk to the guy, Peter, a real piece of work.

(He holds up his index finger.)

I thought I would try to reason with him, man to man. And when you hit someone with a chair, even if it's a few times, you expect him to be hurt but not dead. But he died. And because I loved her so much, each one after him was progressively easier, maybe some were messier, but all of them were easier. Jerry. Charlie. Max.

*(He holds up an additional finger for each name, counting the men off. **DIANE** looks like she might bolt, but **STANLEY** takes her hands, gently.)*

Hear this clearly, let it fill in every little bit of your ears: once you know you can do something, once you know how much you'll risk for love, well…everything gets easier. Because it's what you have to do.

DIANE. Are you telling me [that you…?]

STANLEY. [And I think,] I really do think that I probably saved Tessa from a life of unhappiness and lesser love. I know I did. Like I said, there are people capable of experiencing the full, complex, amazing freedom true love offers. And I think we're both those kinds of people. You and me. And I won't give up. Not even if it seems futile, I'll keep going. In hope, in desperation, in whichever way there is to keep going. Doesn't matter. And I can tell that you won't give up, no matter what you have to do. For Evan.

DIANE. For Evan.

STANLEY. Yes, absolutely yes. So your love can thrive. No matter who you might have to move out of the way.

DIANE. No matter who I might have to move out of the way.

STANLEY. That's right. And all because you love him more than anything, more than anyone ever could and you have to keep him safe.

DIANE. I have to keep him safe.

STANLEY. Yes.

DIANE. Yes.

> (**DIANE** *and* **STANLEY** *continue to look at each other.*)

STANLEY. Do you understand?

DIANE. Yes.

STANLEY. I think you do.

DIANE. I do.

> (**MIRABELLE** *is banging on the door.* **DIANE** *and* **STANLEY** *continue looking at each other. Their gaze is broken when* **EVAN** *passes through the room and throws open the door.*)

EVAN. What?

MIRABELLE. Oh hi, Evan, how are you?

EVAN. Mirabelle

MIRABELLE. You look nice.

> (**EVAN** *does his best to be polite, but it's been a long day.*)

EVAN. What do you want?

MIRABELLE. No hug?

EVAN. Are you kidding?

MIRABELLE. Well, I wasn't kidding but now I don't need a hug from you with that attitude. Your girlfriend is rubbing off on you. You know, you used to have good manners. I remember how good your manners were, I remember it well. You remember how you showed me your good manners.

EVAN. Uh, I don't really [think…]

MIRABELLE. [You] remember.

EVAN. I mean, I [guess, but…]

DIANE. [Holy Christ,] Mirabelle, so he fucked you once, a long time ago. Probably when he was drunk. How long are you going to hold it over his head, my head? Get a fucking clue. No one here has time for you right now.

MIRABELLE. You weren't here, you don't know. Drunk, huh?

EVAN. I was a little drunk.

DIANE. And who even cares if he was stone cold sober? Who cares if he was high on pain medication because his sister just clocked him in the knee with a hammer?

EVAN. Diane!

DIANE. No, no. There are things happening here that are stratospherically more important than you, Mirabelle.

MIRABELLE. Oh really?

DIANE. Really! And whatever happened in the past doesn't make a difference now because it's never happening again.

MIRABELLE. Says you.

DIANE. Says me and everybody! Says me and everybody in the whole wide world ever! And you know what? I'm not the reason it's never happening again, I'm not! And the people in the hall aren't the reason it's never happening again, and the people "banging on the floor" aren't the reason it's never happening again, your stupid stuffed cat isn't even the reason it's never happening again, it's just not gonna' happen. Ask him.

MIRABELLE. I don't have to ask him.

EVAN. It's never happening again.

MIRABELLE. I didn't ask, you don't have to answer something that I [didn't even...]

EVAN. [Mirabelle,] it is never happening again.

(Pause.)

MIRABELLE. Well clearly, maybe, clearly, no maybe I, I might have misjudged the situation. But I was pretty sure I understood, but then I guess I didn't understand what was happening. I didn't, because when we first met you were so nice. So nice to me. And when I watch you in your window at night...that's not what I do. I don't do that. Sometimes my cats go out on the fire escape and if I happen to see you, then... Huh, look at me standing here in the hall, probably in the way. What if someone else needed to get down the hall?

(*She looks at the floor and then at her hands…*)

I'm a hall stander. I'm one of those people. I never thought I was one of those people. I never thought I would be one of those, no. No, no, no no no, no I'm not one of those people, never ever, I'm not, but you're one of those people, you are Diane, with your face and that look, one of those "this is the way it goes" people, one of those "I don't care what you want" people, one of those rude, awful, thieving, manipulative, backstabbing, hateful, disgusting, ugly people that…

(**DIANE** *lets out a roar as she charges* **MIRABELLE**. **EVAN** *is thrown back when his shoulder is hit. The women fight.*)

STANLEY. Diane, maybe you [should…]

DIANE. [Stay out] of it Stanley!

MIRABELLE. You've always been a bitch.

DIANE. And you've always been crazy.

(**EVAN** *drags himself up off the floor.*)

EVAN. You both need to stop this.

MIRABELLE. [Shut-up, Evan!]

DIANE. [Shut-up, Evan!]

STANLEY. (*Looking to* **EVAN**…) Should I try to get her out of here?

MIRABELLE. Oh! So you need your friends to help you out, huh?

DIANE. He's not my friend, he's Ellen's friend Tessa's friend and at least we have friends. What do you have, a fucking stuffed cat?

MIRABELLE. Don't talk about my cat!

(*She throws her stuffed cat at* **DIANE**.)

DIANE. I hope your cat gets its' stuffing pulled out!

MIRABELLE. I will kill you!

> (**MIRABELLE** *and* **DIANE** *start out scratching and clawing at each other, they pull hair, but it is not a generic "cat fight." It is a brawl. Punches are thrown. Blood is drawn. The men are powerless to help. When they try, they are thrown away or accidentally hurt. It is a very long fight. In fact, it goes on way too long. It moves around the room, maybe even into the hall and back. It is ridiculous. It is injurious. It is exhausting. It is all of the violence that has been accumulating underneath the play suddenly bubbling to the surface between these two women. Eventually they get so tired that Evan can get between them. He faces* **MIRABELLE.**)

EVAN. You should go home now.

MIRABELLE. *(collecting her stuffed cat)* She started it.

DIANE. I'll finish it!

EVAN. Diane, haven't we had enough violence for today?

DIANE. I know. I know, it just, it just works its way inside, doesn't it? Under your skin. I can feel it in my hands, all over the apartment, I don't know what I'm doing.

MIRABELLE. No you don't.

> (**EVAN** *turns on her…*)

EVAN. Mirabelle, I'm, look, I'm flattered that you think so much of me, or whatever you think of me, I'm flattered.

MIRABELLE. Good. That's good.

EVAN. And I don't want to be mean to you; I've tried really hard not to [be mean.]

MIRABELLE. [Good. Just be] nice, you're good [at that.]

EVAN. [But you need] to understand that whatever happened that one time isn't worth all of this. I'm in love with Diane, I love her and I'm with her and that's not going anywhere, okay?

MIRABELLE. No, but I thought, I thought [you were…]

EVAN. [I love] her. I don't love you, I love her. You've got to really hear me when I say that I love Diane. I don't want to hurt you, but I don't know how else to say it.

*(**MIRABELLE** is breaking but she won't. She will not.)*

*(**ELLEN** enters with **JEROME**.)*

ELLEN. I'm so sorry. Jerome said I passed out?

JEROME. I did say that, that's what I told her. But it was so loud out here.

EVAN. You should be resting.

DIANE. You should be resting too.

JEROME. I told her.

ELLEN. I feel okay. Oh. Hi, Mirabelle.

MIRABELLE. Hi, Ellen.

ELLEN. Did you want to come in for a minute?

MIRABELLE. [No.]

EVAN. [No.]

STANLEY. [No.]

DIANE. [No.]

ELLEN. All right.

*(**ELLEN** sits on the couch. **JEROME** stands away a bit.)*

STANLEY. Where's Tessa?

JEROME. In there still, where do you think? She didn't, like, climb out the window or anything.

STANLEY. You are so very, very unlikable.

JEROME. No, I'm not.

DIANE. Yes, you are.

STANLEY. Where is she?

ELLEN. She's freshening up. She got over emotional for a minute about my fainting I think. It really scared her. She's so adorable.

MIRABELLE. I need to, I need to get back to my cats. They need me. I'm important to them. I'm important. I have things, important things to do. I matter. And, and you keep the noise down; do you hear me? Keep it down or I'll come back and give you another piece of my mind. And I don't care what any of you say, I know what's what and who's where and how things should go. I do. I do. So, right, don't make me come back because next time I won't be so nice to you, Diane, or your hall standing friends, that's right, that angry guy and that silly little pretty "mam" lady. With her apologies and her nervous smiles, she's lucky I didn't take my fist and pop her [right in the….]

> (**STANLEY** *bristles at the mention of* **TESSA** *and focuses in on* **MIRABELLE**.)

STANLEY. [Why don't] I walk you back to your place Mirabelle?

MIRABELLE. No thank you.

STANLEY. Let me walk you back to your place Mirabelle.

MIRABELLE. No. Thank you.

STANLEY. I'm gonna walk you back to your place.

MIRABELLE. No.

STANLEY. But look…you're still standing here. Diane, remember our chat.

DIANE. I do. I will. I am.

STANLEY. Good. It was pleasure meeting all of you. Let's go.

> (*He leads* **MIRABELLE** *out the door and down the hall.* **EVAN** *closes the door and sits down on the couch next to* **ELLEN**.)

ELLEN. I like that Stanley; he seems like a real "take charge" kind of guy, doesn't he?

DIANE. Yes he does.

JEROME. I can be a "take charge" kind of guy [too.]

> (*They all ignore* **JEROME**.)

EVAN. [You feel] okay?

ELLEN. Don't worry about me, how do you feel?

EVAN. My shoulder aches a little but I'll live.

ELLEN. You can survive anything, huh?

> (**DIANE** *laughs and immediately suppresses it.*)

DIANE. I'm just tired.

(TESSA enters. She looks refreshed.)

TESSA. Needed a quick moment to myself there. How's everyone feeling?

(She notices the messy room.)

Oh…where's Stanley?

DIANE. He's walking Mirabelle to her apartment.

TESSA. The neighbor lady?

EVAN. That's her.

DIANE. I think he just wanted to…smooth things over.

TESSA. He's so considerate. It's really quite astounding isn't it?

EVAN. He's a bigger person than me.

TESSA. He's so kind and he says the sweetest things. Things I don't deserve really.

ELLEN. I'm sure that's not true.

TESSA. I always say I don't know what I'd do without him. I hope I never have to find out. Well look, honey, if everything's okay for now I might just catch up with him? It's been quite an afternoon.

ELLEN. Oh, I'll be okay. I'm just a little tired now. And maybe a bit parched.

(DIANE perks up.)

DIANE. Parched?

ELLEN. Mm hm, parched.

DIANE. I'll, I will get you some lemonade.

(DIANE begins to exit.)

TESSA. Oh Diane, um, we never got to finish our, our "little chat?"

DIANE. I spoke with Stanley. He helped me see things clearly and I feel much better.

TESSA. Do you?

DIANE. You can't imagine. And, uh, Tessa?

TESSA. Yes, honey?

  (pause)

DIANE. It was nice to meet you.

  (DIANE *exits.)*

ELLEN. Thank you for coming Tessa, it was silly to call you. But I'm glad you were here.

TESSA. Me too. Sometimes just having people around can make things better. Evan, I hope you get healed up soon. It was nice to meet you.

EVAN. You too Tessa. When you step out, just follow the hall. It's left, left, left and you'll find Stanley.

TESSA. I'll do that.

JEROME. Bye.

TESSA. Mm hm.

  (She exits.)

EVAN. I'm glad you're feeling better.

ELLEN. I'm glad you're feeling better.

JEROME. I'm gonna go now.

ELLEN. Oh Jerome, what did you want to tell me?

JEROME. Nothing.

  (JEROME *suddenly unravels in a flight of language, a torrent, it's almost amazing that he can even breathe while talking so fast as his body loosens, releasing from the ever-present awkward tension…)*

Ellen, there are these borders or barriers between people, that doesn't do them justice, like these grand meridians that are so much larger than you could, than anyone could ever imagine. Not larger, wider. Between people and we can't even see them and we don't even try mostly. But sometimes, sometimes you pull yourself together and walk up to the edge, you lean out and you look across expecting to see what you always see: the outside of everyone else, which is just the most depressing thing. Not just depressing, that's not bad enough; it's also distant, never close, not really. Even when you're close, physically I mean, right up against each other, what passes for close. Which isn't very close. I'm going.

(He begins to exit, then stops.)

But sometimes Ellen, sometimes if you're lucky, and I'm lucky right now, you see someone standing on the other side looking back. Or you think they're looking back. See enough to believe they're looking back. And that's enough.

(He begins to exit, then stops.)

And Ellen, the idea that you're that person looking back, even if you're not that person, but the fact that you might be is amazing. And, whatever, I know I'm a jerk. And I know I'm not what a lot of people would consider considerate, or even nice, or even maybe tolerable, but I heard you crying on the phone and I came here immediately, automatically, because something in my chest shot into my throat when I heard your voice and pulled me out the door to make sure you were okay. Ellen, I love you and even though I hate Diane and I'm jealous of Evan and annoyed by Evan, sorry Evan, I would never hold that against you. It's painfully perplexing to me, all of this and how you are, but I would never hold that against you. Ever. Because I love you more than I hate anything else.

(He moves towards the couch, looming over her.)

And I can see across that divide, see you looking back, or at least looking this way and I so want to love you that it's enough. You should know that.

> *(Pause. She begins to speak, but he swoops in with a kiss, a deep kiss. At first* **ELLEN** *is surprised, then stiff, then she gives in and swoons.* **EVAN** *looks await and waits for it to end.* **JEROME** *pulls away, satisfied and she is left hanging…)*

And I'm gonna go now.

(He exits quickly before anyone can say anything.
ELLEN *exhales.)*

ELLEN. Whoa. That was a lot.

EVAN. I have no idea what you see in him.

ELLEN. He's not a bad guy.

EVAN. He's kind of a bad guy.

ELLEN. He's just complicated.

EVAN. And at least a little crazy.

ELLEN. Aren't we all?

(She laughs and it's a little crazy.)

It's, when he looks at me, it's like there's no one else in the world for him. I'm all he sees. It feels amazing. And it's a really hard feeling to give up.

EVAN. I think I understand.

ELLEN. I think so, too.

EVAN. But also, sometimes…sometimes you have to loosen your grip on people, just a little bit, so you remember that it's okay. Right?

ELLEN. I know that, silly.

EVAN. Do you?

(Pause. They look at each other. It's deep and anxious.)

ELLEN. We don't have to talk about Jerome, it makes you upset.

EVAN. I wasn't talking about [Jerome, Ellen.]

ELLEN. [No, no, I know] you don't like him.

*(***EVAN*** sighs and relents.)*

EVAN. Okay. Look, all I've ever wanted is for you to be happy. And safe. And if Jerome makes you happy, then I'll try to wrap my head around that.

ELLEN. Good.

EVAN. But promise me you'll keep an open mind about other guys.

ELLEN. Oh Evan.

(They both laugh a bit as she slaps his injured shoulder playfully. She keeps laughing. He winces but smiles through it.)

*(**DIANE** enters with a glass of lemonade. She witnesses the slap. She smoothes herself out a bit, but her hand shakes as she presents it to **ELLEN**.)*

DIANE. Here you go. It took me a minute to find the… sugar.

EVAN. Your hand is shaking?

DIANE. Oh, I'm just exhausted from today, you know?

*(**ELLEN** takes the lemonade. **DIANE** sits and waits…)*

EVAN. So everyone's gone now.

DIANE. You should really drink that, don't want you to dehydrate.

ELLEN. Now that it's so quiet, I can really tell how crazy today actually was.

EVAN. I know what you mean. But we'll all be fine.

DIANE. It's the lemonade you like so much.

EVAN. Let's try to have fewer days like this, all right?

ELLEN. Deal.

EVAN. Deal.

DIANE. Ellen, drink it.

ELLEN. Oh, right. Sorry.

*(She drinks the lemonade. **DIANE** watches her intently and then exhales.)*

DIANE. Good.

ELLEN. Mmm, oh, it tastes funny.

DIANE. Does it?

ELLEN. But it's still good.

DIANE. I love you, Evan.

EVAN. Oh, I love you too, baby.

ELLEN. You two are so sweet. Isn't this nice?

DIANE. It'll be even nicer soon. Lemonade fixes everything.

> *(The* **CROW** *from the prologue flies through the scene and lands in the same area as the top of the play. Lights warm as she lands and the* **FOX** *appears. The lights dim on the apartment,* **ELLEN** *and* **DIANE** *still smiling at each other in the low light, as* **EVAN** *gets up and crosses towards the* **FOX** *and* **CROW**. **EVAN** *becomes the* **NARRATOR** *but remains essentially* **EVAN**. *Again he tells his story. Again the* **FOX** *and the* **CROW** *act it out very simply and cleanly. But this time around, things may break down a bit towards the end.)*

> *(***DIANE** *and* **ELLEN** *watch, intrigued by the tale.)*

NARRATOR. Once there was a Fox.

> *(The* **FOX** *bows.)*

And a Crow.

> *(The* **CROW** *curtseys.)*

And one day, the Fox saw the Crow fly off with a piece of cheese in her beak and settle down nicely on the branch of a tree. The Crow was, of course, going to eat the cheese, as crows are wont to do. But the Fox had a different plan.

FOX. That's for me, as I am a Fox.

NARRATOR. Said the Fox as he swiftly made his way to the foot of the tree.

FOX. Good day to you, Crow.

NARRATOR. He called up to her. And the Crow said nothing.

FOX. How very well you are looking today.

NARRATOR. Said the Fox. And the Crow said nothing.

FOX. How glossy your feathers; how bright your eyes.

NARRATOR. Nothing.

FOX. I feel certain your voice must surpass that of other birds.

NARRATOR. Nothing.

FOX. Just as your fine figure does; let me hear but one song, one joyous, clarion, brilliant, magical song [from you…]

NARRATOR. [Almost as if] she wasn't [even listening.]

FOX. [Let me hear] but one song, one joyous, clarion, brilliant, magical song from you that I may [greet you…]

NARRATOR. [Almost as if] she thought all people were [liars.]

(The **FOX** *quickly snaps at the* **NARRATOR.** *)*

FOX. [Shut-up.]

(The **FOX** *turns back to the* **CROW.** *)*

Let me hear your song.

(The **CROW** *eats the cheese.)*

NARRATOR. And the Crow, uninterested in the overtures of the Fox, enjoyed her cheese, as crows are wont to do.

CROW. That will do nicely.

NARRATOR. Said the Crow.

FOX. I don't know what to do, this has never happened before.

NARRATOR. Said the Fox.

CROW. I do love some delicious cheese.

NARRATOR. Said the Crow.

FOX. I'm leaving.

NARRATOR. Said the Fox.

(The **FOX** *waits for a reaction.)*

FOX. I said I'm leaving.

NARRATOR. Said the Fox again.

FOX. Fine.

(The **FOX** *begins to leave.)*

NARRATOR. Said the Fox as he sulked away into the forest with his tail between his legs.

FOX. I'm not skulking!

(*The* **FOX** *skulks away.*)

NARRATOR. And thus the Crow was left alone on her branch in her tree.

CROW. It's better this way in the end.

NARRATOR. Said the Crow and who could blame her, really? Especially given the possible alternatives.

(*He references* **DIANE** *and* **ELLEN** *on the couch.*)

CROW. Exactly.

NARRATOR. Said the Crow.

CROW. This is a much better than that other one.

NARRATOR. She said as she quietly sat, happy, humming a little tune…

(*The* **CROW** *hums a little tune.*)

Happy to not interact with the other, crafty, scheming animals, happy to have a belly full of delicious cheese that she didn't have to share, happy to have not heard nice things if they weren't true in the end, happy to have not learned a lesson that involved losing something precious.

CROW. Wait a minute.

NARRATOR. Happy to spend her days never trying to connect with others for fear that they might lie, that she might be cheated or damaged beyond repair.

CROW. Wait just one [minute.]

NARRATOR. [Happier than] if she was to take a chance and reach out to someone even though it might end in hurt or heartbreak. Because it's always scarier to take a chance.

CROW. Stop that, [stop it.]

NARRATOR. [So it's] that kind of moral to the story; that kind of "happy."

CROW. Don't say it like that. I am happy.

NARRATOR. Said the Crow to the Narrator.

CROW. I'm quite happy.

NARRATOR. And lonely.

CROW. Happy.

NARRATOR. And lonely.

CROW. Happy.

NARRATOR. Lonely.

CROW. No, happy. Happy. Happy!

NARRATOR. She insisted to herself. And somewhere inside, she tried awfully hard to believe it.

> *(The* **CROW** *and the* **NARRATOR** *turn their attention towards* **DIANE** *and* **ELLEN** *sitting on the couch.)*

> *(***DIANE** *and* **ELLEN** *look at each other.* **ELLEN** *abruptly and quietly seizes up, a quick thing: she looks at the glass, she looks at a wide-eyed* **DIANE** *and then she falls limp on the couch. The empty glass drops from her hand and rolls across the floor.* **DIANE** *is very still. Then she exhales and smiles.)*

> *(blackout)*

End of Play

9 780573 704598